Alfie's Trumpeting Troubles

Written by Janet Sullivan Wiggins
Illustrated by Joni-Leigh Doran

ISBN: 978-1-945190-60-5

For Trich and Ofentsé,
who introduced me to the wonderful
world of elephants.

Alfie, the little elephant, lived in the African savanna where the tall grasses grow. Alfie lived with his mother, his brothers, his sisters and aunts.

Alfie loved grazing on grasses, nibbling on fruit, and splishing and splashing in streams in the spring.

As long as Alfie was busy foraging for food
with his family, everything was quiet. But
when the little fellow was feeling frisky and
a tiny bit bored, it was time to hang on
to your hat, for Alfie was a naughty little

elephant who loved to lumber along and

trumpet to astound the animals all around.

He trumpeted throughout the day, and he

trumpeted all through the night for as long

and as loud as he could.

His mother bellowed, "Stop! Alfie, stop!"
His brothers and sisters bellowed,
"Stop! Alfie, stop!" and even the jaunty
giraffes and the other animals were totally
befuddled. But the more they asked Alfie,
the more he trumpeted and even louder and
longer.

The ground rattled, the leaves on the trees
blew, the bushes shook and all the animals ran
twisting and turning in every direction. When
Alfie saw them all scatter, he rolled and he
romped around on the ground, rollicking and
roaring with laughter.

After rollicking, romping and rolling, Alfie spotted a lovely lanky giraffe who was dining on leaves from the tops of the trees. It was then he decided to try his trunk at trumpeting. Little did he know that not only was she lovely and lanky, but she was also crafty and cunning.

The giraffe shouted, "You naughty noisy elephant! You're perturbing and disturbing the animals all over the grand savanna!" Alfie giggled and laughed, "Ha ha, he he, ho ho hurmph" and again he tried to trumpet.

"Just keep laughing little elephant, as long as you can," the giraffe sighed as she shrugged and smiled, "but you have just trumpeted ONE time too many!"

And as soon as she said it, the crafty giraffe concocted a plan to stop the annoying Alfie. She gathered her friends from far and near, "Come with me, my dear friends." she exclaimed! "The trick has to be the fabulous fruit of the great and mighty marula." For you see, the fruit of that tree, can make a naughty noisy elephant ever so, ever so, sleepy.

It didn't take long for the giraffe and her friends to find a mighty marula that was covered in fabulous fruit. The crafty giraffe stretched her long neck and plucked the fruit from that tree. After gathering the treats, the giraffe and her friends all chuckled and giggled and laughed as they said, "This grand little plan should fool that NOT so funny fellow!" Then they marched along through the sunny savanna scattering the fruit around and about where Alfie loved to trumpet.

The crafty giraffe and her friends then hid behind some tall grasses, and it didn't take long for the scent of that fruit to waft its way to Alfie. Alfie sniffed and he snuffed and followed his trunk until he found those tasty treats.

"Chomp chomp, chomp chomp, chomp chomp," Up they went from his long grey trunk and into his munching mouth. And down they tumbled and traveled into his hungry tummy.

After Alfie had munched and crunched and hurumphed, he began to feel quite full. He felt frisky and funny and decided to try his trunk at trumpeting. But as soon as he tried, he tripped as he trumpeted and fell fast asleep beside the treats from that tree.

He dreamed as he dozed of eating millions of fruit and of never-ending trumpeting, but all that came out of that troublesome trunk was a sweet little, "tweet, tweet, tweet!" So when Alfie awoke and thought of his dream, he finally agreed, "I'll never again need to trumpet."

As the years went by and Alfie grew older, his mother, his brothers, his sisters, his aunts, and the crafty giraffe and her friends could hardly remember the time, long ago, when they ever had to shout, " Stop! Alfie, stop!" as he trumpeted louder and louder and longer. So whenever they greeted the dear young fellow, the crafty giraffe and her friends joined in and chanted, "Hello, Alfie, hello. It's so good to see you QUIET friend!"

Even today the animals still laugh and play where the tall grasses grow. They rollick and roll and frolick together.

Now Alfie, the elephant, tries his trunk at hugging and hugging and loving his mother, his brothers, his sisters, his aunts and all of his animal friends, instead of all his troublesome trumpeting.

About the Author

Janet Wiggins is a native Floridian, but she lived in Texas where she raised her family and taught primary grades for many years. After retiring, she relocated to the eastern shore of Mobile Bay near her roots in Pensacola, Florida.

She has previously written "Miss Millicent Monarch… a Butterfly's Tale", which tells about the metamorphosis and migration of the monarch butterfly.

She continues to follow her passions by volunteering in her community, traveling, watercolor painting and photography.

About the Illustrator

Joni-Leigh Doran was born and raised in South Africa, where she formally trained as a graphic designer and illustrator. She also works as a fine artist, and her love of the wilderness and it's inhabitants is one of her greatest sources of inspiration.

She currently lives on a farm in a coastal town of the Western Cape in South Africa with her partner Ian and their beloved horse and golden retriever.

 facebook.com/DesignerJoni    jonileighdoran